walnut
squirrel
cottonwood
sweetgum
cirrus

for Sondy, who always knows just what to do.

Farrar Straus Giroux Books for Young Readers
An imprint of Macmillan Publishing Group, LLC
120 Broadway, New York, NY 10271

Color separations by Bright Arts (H.K.) Ltd.
Printed in China by RR Donnelley Asia Printing Solutions Ltd.,
Dongguan City, Guangdong Province
Designed by Aram Kim
First edition, 2020
10 9 8 7 6 5 4 3 2 1

mackids.com

Library of Congress Cataloging-in-Publication Data is available
ISBN: 978-0-374-31252-7

Our books may be purchased in bulk for promotional, educational, or business use. Please contact your local bookseller or the Macmillan Corporate and Premium Sales Department at (800) 221-7945 ext. 5442 or by email at MacmillanSpecialMarkets@macmillan.com.

Anything with You

Charlie Mylie

Farrar Straus Giroux
New York

look!

let's do something together.

you and me.

let's see what we find.

let's see where this takes us.

with you,

there's always a way.

you know just what to do.

what would I do without you?

let's keep going.

you and me.

with you,

I always feel better.

look!

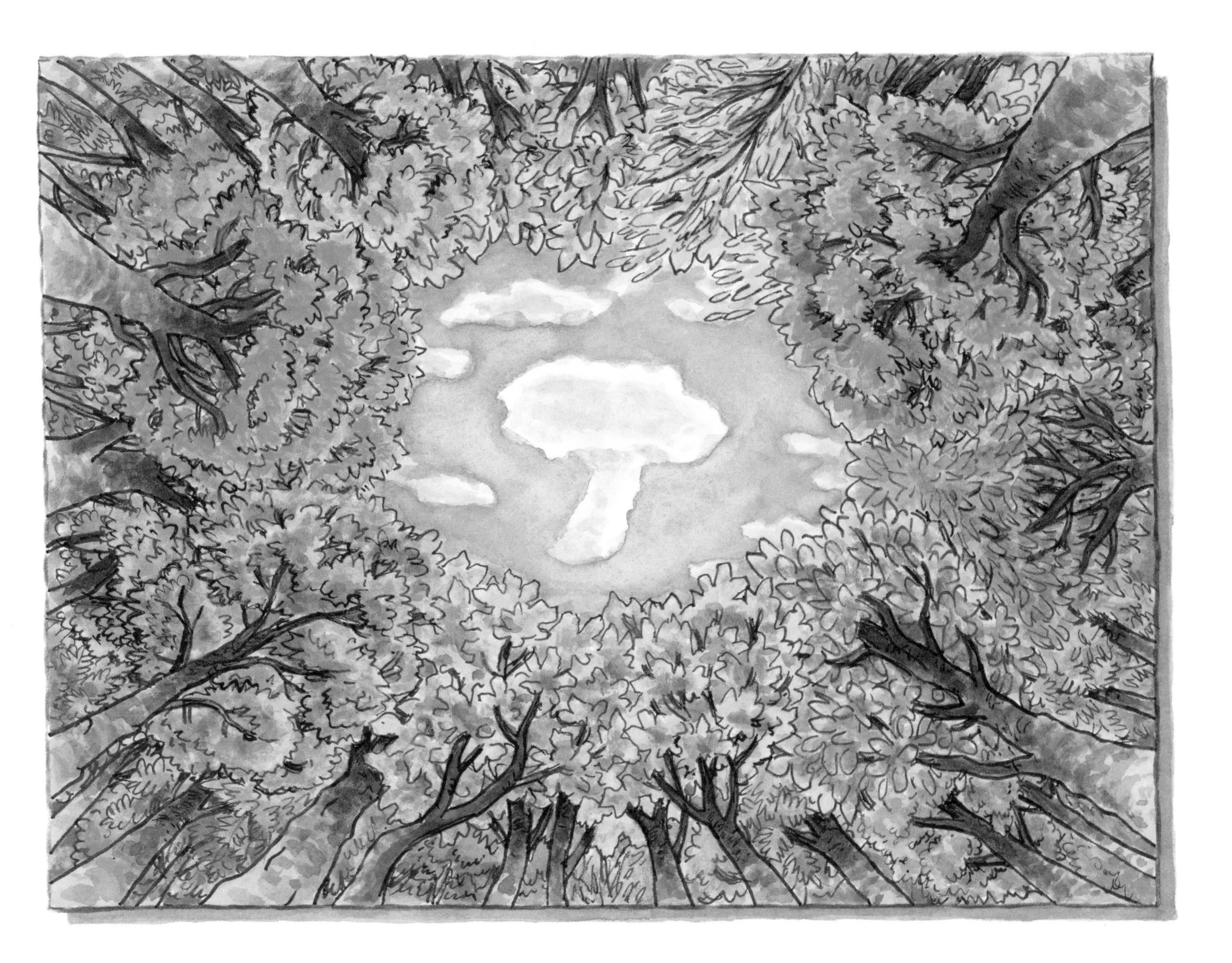

it's time to head home.

hold on to what we have

and smile at what we found.

red eared slider
oak
woolly bear
stratus
oyster
beetle